Dear Parents,

Welcome to the Scholastic Reader series. We have taken over 80 years of experience with teachers, parents, and children and put it into a program that is designed to match your child's interests and skills.

Level 1—Short sentences and stories made up of words kids can sound out using their phonics skills and words that are important to remember.

Level 2—Longer sentences and stories with words kids need to know and new "big" words that they will want to know.

Level 3—From sentences to paragraphs to longer stories, these books have large "chunks" of texts and are made up of a rich vocabulary.

Level 4—First chapter books with more words and fewer pictures.

It is important that children learn to read well enough to succeed in school and beyond. Here are ideas for reading this book with your child:

- Look at the book together. Encourage your child to read the title and make a prediction about the story.
- Read the book together. Encourage your child to sound out words when appropriate. When your child struggles, you can help by providing the word.
- Encourage your child to retell the story. This is a great way to check for comprehension.
- Have your child take the fluency test on the last page to check progress.

Scholastic Readers are designed to support your child's efforts to learn how to read at every age and every stage. Enjoy helping your child learn to read and love to read.

         —Francie Alexander
           Chief Education Officer
           Scholastic Education

For Tara and Joshua
—E.H.T.

For Langford Outlaw
—J.M.

Text copyright © 1974 by Edith Tarcov.
Illustrations copyright © 1974 by James Marshall.
Activities copyright © 2003 Scholastic Inc.

All rights reserved. Published by Scholastic Inc.
SCHOLASTIC, CARTWHEEL BOOKS, and associated logos are trademarks
and/or registered trademarks of Scholastic Inc.

Library of Congress Cataloging-in-Publication Data is available.

ISBN 0-590-46571-6

19 20 21 22   11 12 13 14/0

Printed in the U.S.A.   40

First printing, June 1993

The Frog Prince

Retold by Edith H. Tarcov

Illustrated by James Marshall

Scholastic Reader — Level 3

Cartwheel
·B·O·O·K·S·®

SCHOLASTIC INC.

New York   Toronto   London   Auckland   Sydney
Mexico City   New Delhi   Hong Kong   Buenos Aires

Once upon a time there was a beautiful princess. She had a golden ball, and it was her favorite plaything. She took it wherever she went.

One day the princess was
playing in the woods, near a
well. She threw her ball high
into the air.

It fell — **splash!** — into
the well.

The princess watched her
golden ball sink deep into the
water of the well, and she
began to cry. She cried harder
and harder.

Suddenly someone said,
"What is the matter, princess?
Why are you making so much
noise?"

The princess looked around. She looked into the well.

An ugly little frog was looking up at her. The frog asked again, "What is the matter, princess?"

"Oh, it's you, you old water-splasher," the princess said. "My golden ball has fallen into the well. That is why I am crying."

"Stop crying," said the frog. "Maybe I can help you. What will you give me if I get your ball for you?"

"I will give you whatever you want, dear frog," said the princess. "Would you like my fine silk dress? Or my necklace of pearls? Or would you like my golden crown?"

"No," said the frog. "What would I do with your fine silk dress? Or your necklace of pearls?

"And what would I do with your golden crown?"

"What do you want, then?" the princess asked.

The frog looked at the beautiful princess.

He said, "I want to be your friend and playmate. I want to sit with you at the supper table. I want to eat with you from your golden plate and drink with you from your golden cup. I want to sleep on your fine silk pillow. If you promise to let me do these things, I will get your ball for you."

"I promise," the princess said.

She thought, how can this nasty little frog come to the castle and be my playmate? He has to stay here, in his well. And she said again, "I promise."

Now the frog went down, deep into the well. Soon he came up with the golden ball in his mouth. He threw it onto the grass.

"Oh!" said the princess.
"My golden ball!" She picked it
up and ran away.

"Wait, wait!" cried the frog.
"Take me with you! I can't go
as fast as you!"

But the princess did not
wait. She ran home to the
castle. And soon she forgot all
about the poor little frog.

The next day, at supper time, the princess sat at the table with her father the king and all the people of the court.

Suddenly everyone heard some strange noises outside.

Splish, splash, splish, splash!

It was the sound of wet little feet coming up the stairs to the castle.

Then,

Flip, flap, flip, flap!

There was a slippery little knock at the door. Someone called:

**"Princess, princess,
open up!
Princess, princess,
let us sup!"**

The princess ran to the door and opened it.

When she saw the frog, she
shut the door quickly.

The princess came running back to the table. The king looked at her.

"What are you afraid of, Daughter?" he asked. "Is there a giant at the door who wants to carry you off?"

"Oh no, Father," said the princess. "It is not a giant. It's a nasty little frog."

The princess told her father how the frog had found her ball. And she told him about her promise.

"I promised I would let him be my friend and playmate," she said. "But I never thought he could come out of the well!"

Flip, flap, flip, flap!

There was that slippery
little knock again. And someone
called:

"Princess, princess,
open up!
Princess, princess,
let us sup!
Remember who brought
you the ball that fell!
Remember your promise
by the well!"

"You must keep your promise, Daughter," said the king. "Open the door and let the frog in."

And so the princess had to open the door.

The frog hopped in and followed her to the table. He stopped by her chair.

"Pick me up and put me next to your plate," said the frog.

"Go ahead," the king said. "Do as the frog says. You must keep your promise."

The princess had to put the
frog on the table.

Everyone could see that she
really did not want to do it.

The frog ate with the
princess from her golden plate.
And he drank with her from
her golden cup. The frog liked
his supper very much. But the
princess could not eat a thing.

At last the frog said, "Now I am ready to go to sleep. Carry me to your bedroom. And put me on your fine silk pillow."

The princess began to cry.

"Stop crying," said the king. "Do as the frog says. You made a promise, and you must keep it!"

And so the princess had to carry the frog to her bedroom. She took hold of him with two fingers, and she put him in a corner.

But the frog said, "I am tired. I want to go to sleep on a fine bed, just like you. Put me on your silk pillow, or I will tell your father."

That made the princess very angry.

She picked up the frog, and she threw him against the wall!

But when he fell to the floor, the frog was no longer a frog.

Now he was a tall prince with beautiful, kind eyes. And he was smiling at the princess.

"A wicked witch turned me into a frog," he said. "But now the spell is broken!"

The very next day the
prince and the princess were
married.

A golden coach with eight white horses drove up to the castle. The prince now took the princess to his own land. And they lived there happily forever after.

The End